— An Aborted —
AMBITIOUS
GOAL

— An Aborted —
AMBITIOUS
GOAL

Marie L. Cassagnol

AN ABORTED AMBITIOUS GOAL

iUniverse books may be ordered through booksellers or by contacting:

iUniverse
1663 Liberty Drive
Bloomington, IN 47403
www.iuniverse.com
844-349-9409

Because of the dynamic nature of the internet, any web addresses or links contained in this book may have changed since publication and may no longer be valid. The views expressed in this work are solely those of the author and do not necessarily reflect the views of the publisher, and the publisher hereby disclaims any responsibility for them.

Any people depicted in stock imagery provided by Getty Images are models, and such images are being used for illustrative purposes only. Certain stock imagery © Getty Images.

ISBN: 978-1-6632-2527-6 (sc)
ISBN: 978-1-6632-2528-3 (e)

Library of Congress Control Number: 2021912950

Print information available on the last page.

iUniverse rev. date: 03/14/2022

PREFACE

I wrote this short story to kill time after one of my brothers passed away. I worked on it, and now *An Aborted Ambitious Goal* has become the hottest story I have ever written. I started concentrating on writing when I found out my brother was brutally murdered in Haiti, in 2010, to block the suffering and grief I had endured over his loss. It's still painful today. My goal in this short story is to let readers know that faith is a powerful virtue. This virtue allowed me to find peace within myself and leave everything in the Lord's hands. I know for sure He will bring me justice.

All of a sudden, some ideas came to my mind, and I thought, *I got it*. It is an exciting short story full of surprises. The story line is based on fiction, but it was inspired by true events. It is about sadness, falling from grace, and being blessed again with faith and happiness. *An Aborted Ambitious Goal* is a fictional short story. A lady named Sofia faithfully searched for her daughter, Sofa, for almost two years. She lived in Senegal. Sofia was a true Christian, and Sofa was raised in the same manner. Sofia thought her daughter was abducted. By the grace of God, some of the criminal's family members helped to solve the case by notifying their teachers.

ACKNOWLEDGEMENTS

Thanks to everyone who helped me on my book writing journey!

I am grateful to the publishing company iUniverse. Publisher Marty Cain, editors Jeremy Carey, Courtney Wallace, Author Solutions Hailey Alison, who took a chance on my first book. Thank you very much!

I acknowledge Mr. Pierre VClervil for motivating me throughout the process of publishing my book. You are appreciated! A special thanks to my cousins Sevedieu Pierre and his wife Marie Annette Pierre for listening to my book idea and immediately believing in my success. Their kindness, assistance and compassion helped me to complete my book to accomplish my Goal. Love you both! My gratitude to my nieces Marly P. Lee, Christelle

Ridore, and Moudelonde L. Louis who supported me throughout the process. Love you all! And Mr. Zublair Stephen Honolulu the managing director of the St Lulu Ventures in Nig. Ltd. who always put me in his prayers. My appreciation! I thank my best friend Mireille Boyer who worked vigorously for my goal to become reality. Lastly, my family of course particularly Brendan, Tristan, Zaylan, Kaydan and Syra who can't wait to see my book. Love you all!

CHAPTER 1

The Senegalese were opened to various religions, and the religious practices in Senegal were diverse. Freedom of religion was enclosed in the constitution, and the various religious groups coexisted in relative harmony. The Senegalese believed in supernatural forces, and doctors, herbalists, diviners, and marabous had the power to use these forces.

For Independence Day, the Senegalese enjoyed a yummy yassa onion sauce dish instead of their thieboudienne national dish for lunch, which is fish stuffed with herbs and served with rice and vegetables. It was the best way to celebrate the Senegalese tradition. Cultivation played a big

1

role in the lives of the Senegalese, so they didn't import foods. They preferred to sell their own dairy products made from the milk of local cattle instead of importing milk powder from other countries.

In Dakar, the capital, they also had croissants and pastries for breakfast. The most common drink was called the bissap, which was made from hibiscus, sugar, and water. They imported ginger, a popular juice, as was bouyi, a thick, sugary drink made from the fruit of the baobab. The main meals were made of rice dishes, couscous, and millet. These formed the basis of many dishes, with protein provided by meat, peanuts, or fish. People gathered around their TVs to watch a big wrestling match, and the neighborhood looked for that event to drum and chant all night. They also organized a parade as part of the tradition.

The celebration included closing schools for two weeks. Some people traveled to visit family and friends. I chose Senegal for the setting of my story because the name sounded elegant and sophisticated, marked by a lack of simplicity. Language, culture, history, people, clothing, tradition—its etiquette went along with it. I should say *complex.*

Quintessential represents the most perfect of typical examples of a quinsy or class. This was how I perceived Senegal. The Republic of Senegal was the official name, and French was the official language. Only one quarter of the Senegalese who went to colonial-style schools spoke French. Most people spoke the Wolof—their own ethnic language. Beside the Wolof, there were five major languages: the Server, Appular, Mandinka, Diola, and Dessert. Senegal was a tropical country, surrounded by huge mountains, vast plains, gigantic trees, and clear rivers that flowed into the ocean. Senegal was typically hot and humid, with a rainy season between May and November. It had a strong southeast wind, and a dry season occurred between December and April, dominated by dry, fasten winds. The Senegalese mostly dressed like the French, wearing T-shirts with slogans. Few women were veiled. Some women preferred to wear headdresses with their colorful and traditional billowing touts.

In business, greetings were unnecessary and even wasteful to the Senegalese. When making business cards, they made sure one side of the card was translated in French, and the title was prominently displayed. Cards should be presented with one hand and received with two hands. The Senegalese used a lot of proverbs, especially if what they had to say was delicate in nature.

Communications began after inquiries into the health and well-being of the other person, and they remained positively in the family. They used positive languages so they could demonstrate polite manners and a communicative style at all times. It was very important to greet the Senegalese upon each meeting by not asking them about their wealth and their well-being, which was considered rude. Greetings were used by the Senegalese to feel one with each other and achieve a sense of group harmony. Close friends preferred to hug each other rather than shake hands. Some religious men and women might not shake hands with the opposite sex. They did not consider big gifts as a part of the Senegalese culture. Small gifts were given when someone was invited for a small meal. For example, they could bring a box of chocolates, French pastries, or a nicely packaged fresh fruit. The Senegalese table manners were formal. One had to wait to be shown to their seat, and they would be brought to a basin to wash their hands before the meal was served. Men and women often ate in separate rooms, sometimes in the same room.

CHAPTER 2

In the 1960s, a lady named Sofia and her family were living in Senegal, a small West African country. Their village was located sixty-five miles from the capital, Dakar. It was a member of the French community—approximately 76,124 square miles, with a population of 2.5 million. Dakar is the seaport of Senegal, the largest city among them, totaling 234,000 square miles, with a population over 1 million. Dakar is located on the Cape Verde Peninsula of the Atlantic coast, and it is the westernmost point of the African mainland. Senegal was a French-speaking country, with some Arabic and English speakers. The French occupied Senegal for three centuries, and

Senegal and the French Sudan were granted independence on April 4, 1960. They formed the Federation of Mali. Four months later, the two former colonies decided to become independent nations, and on August 19, 1960, the federation was dissolved. Senegal became its own country. Leopold Sedar Senghor became the first president of Senegal, and he served until 2001.

Sofia met her husband while she was going to school in the neighborhood in which they used to live. At first her family didn't think highly of him, but as time went on they accepted him. Right after they graduated high school, they got married. Nine months later, Sofia gave birth to a beautiful baby girl named Sofa.

Three years later they started having marital problems. Sofia's family should have followed their first instincts because Sofia's husband was the most selfish man alive. They were poor. Sofa never knew her father very well. The relationship between her mother and her father had turned sorrowful after her mother caught him cheating with one of her best friends in her own bed. Although it was acceptable for a man to have three or more wives, according to their religious beliefs, Sofia never agreed to this lifestyle.

Sofa trusted her best friend with her husband, but that trust did not last because her best friend had her best interests in mind instead of Sofia.

Sofia had so many friends, but there was a friend who was very close to her among them, there was one in particular who was friendly. On a Tuesday, she came to their house unannounced. She rang their bell and pushed her way through. the door sat next to her husband without any regard for her best friend Sofia. She started rubbing her elbow on him. This was how deception stepped in.

On a hot summer night, sitting on the beach contemplating the sunset in his trouser, reflecting on the surface of the ocean. I was waiting for my husband to meet me for a romantic night. Unexpectedly, the day retreated to go back to the firmament. In the silence of the night, I saw the moon shining her blue rays over the stream, slowly in her serpentine way, flowing into the sea. Along the seashore the night calm in its coat and comes to play with the stream. All of a sudden, the weather changed and I said to myself, "Is it true? "Is he forgetting?" Then the sound of the stream waves blew so hard and the shadows of the trees gave me the impression that my husband was behind me. Disappointed and saddened, I headed home. When I arrived there, it was too much to handle, I found my husband in bed with one of my best friends. I went outside head down watching them leave. I overlapped, and brought with me the scars of deception unintentionally. Finally, I realized that I have been betrayed by two people who were very dear to me who were gone in an instant just because of a moment of weakness.

Being deceived is very hard especially, when the person who betrays you means the world to you. It is always good to count on your friends especially, when you are having some difficult moments in life. For example, when you are dealing with family matters, financial crisis, and health problems. For a friend to choose one of those financial crisis to betray you, it is not easy.

At the age of three, Sofa's father left Senegal to look for a better life. He never returned. Sofia had no luck with men. When Sofa's father left Senegal, Sofia was in a relationship with another man. The relationship did not turn out so well for her. Sofia was beaten almost every day, and she was verbally abused by him. The man treated her like dirt just because she was not capable of securing their financial stability by finding a good job in Senegal. One day she said enough was enough, and she left him.

The breakup motivated Sofa and pushed her to think of doing something big for herself. Sofa studied hard and worked her way into becoming the youngest fashion designer in her hometown by the age of fourteen. Sofa's goal was to become a supermodel. Her goal could not materialize in Senegal, so she decided to go to the capital to look for modeling jobs. When Sofa felt things were not going her way, she turned to her grandmother, who would do whatever she could to put her on the right track.

The night Sofa moved away from home, her grandma was the first person to know about it and tried to convince her to look back on her decision. Sofa bluntly refused and followed her own instincts. Sofia opposed the idea, thinking it was too dangerous to be in the crazy world. She was worried about Sofa. Sofa's boyfriend opposed the idea too. They had an argument about it that almost turned into a fight, but they kissed and made up. Even so, her decision remained the same.

Sofa did not sleep at all that night, she was thinking about her boyfriend that she loves very much and what would happen while she was away? As she already made her decision not to stay, she did not look back, but with a broken heart. Sofa swore not to leave her boyfriend who is very handsome. Could she prevent what would happen in her life? Only God can predict the future so she had nothing to do, but leaving it in His hands.

Sofa's boyfriend was everything a girl needed in a relationship: sincere, respectful, lovely, honest, and so on. When Sofa left Senegal, some girls from the neighborhood were constantly after him. He was always true to himself, and he told them that until he knew what happened to Sofa his love for her remained the same. Even though it was painful for Sofa to leave her mom and her boyfriend of two years, she had to go.

The next day, Sofa left a note for her mother. She sneaked out in the middle of the night and went to Dakar. Her intention was to return home within a week. When the week was over, Sofia waited all night—no sight of Sofa. At about five o'clock in the morning, Sofia fell asleep and woke up at midday. Sofia was thinking how tired

Sofa must be, or she probably found a job in the capital and would not come home. Sofa did not sleep at all that night...

Sofia was raised in a Christian family. Her father worked as a head electrician for a big company, and her mother was a dressmaker. They never made enough money to support a family of six. The two older children had to work after school to help with the bills, and Sofia and her older brother fit that bill. Sofia's older brother was a gentleman. He spent time with his siblings like they were his own children. He treated his mother with love and respect. He was the kind of brother everybody wished to have. Sofia's mother was strict when it came to raising her children. At all times she made sure they were on their best behavior. Their father, on the other hand, was more flexible. For example, if they wanted to go out, they went to their father first. After getting his approval, they went to tell their mother that their father allowed them to go out. Their mother always insisted he should consult her first before making any decision on letting the children go anywhere because she thought it took two to raise children.

13

Back in the day, they had a hard time communicating over the phone with someone. The best way to communicate with someone was to send someone else over on horse carts or on a carriage, which could take three to four days to reach its destination. Sofia counted the days, wondering what had happened to Sofa. She endured sleepless nights for about six months, and she decided her best bet was to travel to Dakar to search for her.

Sofia traveled for three days on a horse cart.

During Sofia's strict upbringing, there was nobody like Uncle Bill. Whenever they heard him at the door, it seemed like everybody lost their tongues. A sense of calm wrapped around the house, like they just relocated, and no operable device was in it. He was a retired pastor, and they gave him a nickname: Scary Bill.

Every Sunday after church, he always dropped off some boxes labeled with their name, and no one would dare touch them until he left the house. Uncle Bill used to support them with everything that he could—food, clothing, and utilities. He even worked on his brother-in-law's car. Whenever he came to their house he called them one after the other. He questioned them about their school, looked at their skin, and talked to them about each church service that they attended. Then he shook the boy's hands and hugged the girls.

Scary Bill's nieces and nephews asked why he never got married. A source told them that he fell in love with a girl when he was in his early twenties. By mistake, the girl got pregnant. Her family thought Scary Bill was too poor to let him marry her, after she gave birth to a baby boy, her parents took the baby and sent her to a convent. Scary Bill said he used to send money to them to take care of the boy. After a while they relocated, and Scary Bill never knew what became of them. Scary Bill was in a relationship with two other girls. These relationships did not turn out very well. He then decided to go to a theology school. He graduated as a pastor, and from then on he gave himself to God.

Scary Bill never married. One Sunday after church, Uncle Bill had chest pain, and he was taken to the hospital for observation. He spent three months in the hospital. While he was there, he suffered a massive heart attack and died soon after. Even though his nieces and nephews were scared of him, they felt sad because deep down they knew

Uncle Bill was a good person. And they couldn't pinpoint the reason they were scared of him. When they read Uncle Bill's will, he left a car for his sister and a piece of land and some money in the bank for his nieces and nephews. He left a house for Sofia. He made sure they were very well-off after his passing, and they were very grateful for all he had done.

I perceive life in a way not anyone can see it. To me, there are three important words in life that can make an impact on people: respect for others, humility and truthfulness. Sofia proved to everyone she processed those qualities people in Dakar loved that in her. She devoted all her life for her daughter Sofa's well-being and wished that she could be successful in life. She was hoping her effort and determination could pay upfront.

Scary Bill's loved child came to town after he passed away. He brought a lawsuit against the Lagrange family and claimed everything that Scary Bill left behind belonged to him. Unfortunately, the judge found him unfit to claim his inheritance because he had left town when he was fifteen years old and returned in his fifties. During these years, the boy never wrote or visited Scary Bill. He did not know anything about him. At the trial, he became hostile and very disrespectful toward the judge. The judge kept him in jail for thirty days—one day for each year he spent out of his father's life. After his release, he left town and disappeared, the same way he had done in his youth.

CHAPTER 3

When Sofia arrived, she did not waste any time. She rented a room for three dollars a month. Sofia brought some of Sofa's pictures to the police department. They passed them out immediately. Her big dilemma was to locate some of the fashion agencies to start her search.

In Dakar, Sofia met people who welcomed her with open arms. They made sure that she was comfortable, and brought her the most expensive thing that they could afford. Sofia is a very beautiful woman, wherever she goes she finds men who want to be in a relationship with her. But in the situation she was in, she stayed loyal to her daughter Sofa. Sofia's dream was to locate her. She turned them down each time. Life can put you in places that you really don't want to go, but sometimes the destinations can really make your life better. That was exactly what happened in the case of Sofia and daughter Sofa.

After three weeks of living in Dakar, Sofia had no money left. She had no choice but to look for a job. Sofia started looking for jobs, while still searching for Sofa. One day Sofia went to the supermarket to look for a job. The owner of the store offered her a job to take care of her elderly mother. Sofia moved to the old lady's house. She did not pay rent. Sofia saved the money she made to pay for the ongoing investigations. Miss Lily, the old lady she cared for, treated her with respect, and the respect was mutual.

CHAPTER 4

On December 23, 1960, a few teachers reported to the police department that some students from their school notified them about some bad activities allegedly occurring in the mansion of a man named Allicobe and his friends. On the other hand, the teachers were hesitant to bring the complaints forward, as these men were bad news. Allicobe, the richest man in Dakar, thought no one could face him, because he was very powerful, and he had a way to bring people under his wings. Unfortunately, he was wrong.

A year later, after the complaints were investigated, a police officer went to the place where Sofia worked.

Allicobe was served with papers to appear in court the next month. The entire crew was in a state of shock when the police officers entered the Allicobe mansion with a warrant. Even though they knew they had a bad reputation in the capital, they didn't expect the police officers to come through Ally's front door.

Sofia kept in touch with Sofa's boyfriend and her five siblings over the years. She invited them to come to Dakar to assist with the trial.

When the police department checked with Allicobe, he knew from the start that his sons and daughters had something to do with it. They questioned him all the time about the activities that occurred in his mansion. He kicked them out right away. According to the court documents, Allicobe hired drifters to do the dirty jobs for him. For example, people with no self-esteem who were able to gleefully kidnap boys and girls in a flash. Some of the girls knew what they were bargained for because they followed the drifters to get the job.

When Sofa reached her destination, she was wandering the streets of Dakar. A strange man approached her and offered hospitality. He happened to be one of Allicobe's drifters.

Her arrival at the mansion was warm and welcoming. Allicobe hired her right away. She had all the qualities he wanted in an escort—beautiful, smart, tall, with curly long hair. Sofa was forced to work for Allicobe as an escort. She was never allowed to leave the camp by herself and was always escorted by aggressive bodyguards.

Unknown to anyone, they also found out that Sofa's father was one of Allicobe's rich friends. Sofa was scheduled to be introduced to her father. He did not recognize her. Luckily, when she got in his room, her name reminded him of her. She was sent out by her father right away. He called Allicobe to tell him that he did not use her because of her name. When he realized she could be the daughter he abandoned long ago in Senegal, he disappeared until a police officer picked him up for questioning.

Sofa's father was in a common-law marriage with a lady he met in Dakar. She also was Allicobe's accomplice. Sofa was not the only girl working for Allicobe. There were twelve in all. When a girl wanted out of Allicobe's job, Sofa's father's girlfriend reported her to Allicobe. She was severely beaten by him. Since he hired a doctor and a nurse to treat them, he had no problem getting away with the mistreatment they were suffering at his hands.

Arriving in Dakar, Sofa's five siblings, her boyfriend, grandmother and her grandfather went to visit the Dakar's Historic sites before the trial began. Dakar Historic sites are the most visited sites in the whole world. They visited Goree Island, well designed, and explored the impression that everything was real or fascinating. They also visited the IFan Museum, which has a magnificent interior decoration with sculpture portraits of the ancient era Africa. One of Sofa's siblings met a guy at the Museum who wanted to know her she was shy to accept his friendship, but with the approval of her big sister Sofa, she accepted. They had fun.

Ally built a chapel and hired two fake priests. He also built a restaurant and a theater. When a girl wanted to get married to a client, he had to make sure he had the couple sign a contract so the girl could keep working for him. If the couple failed to sign the contract, they couldn't get married. Before sending the girls to work, Ally ordered the bodyguards to pick them up from the camp and have them brought to the restaurant, where they could be cozy with the clients, and then one by one they left the restaurant. He did the same thing for them when he organized a ball at the theatre. Although he understood the devastating effects of his actions, he did it anyway because his greed didn't allow him to stop. It was a very sad situation that they were in, but only God had the last word.

One of the other girls was served a cocktail that sent her to the hospital for two weeks. Any doctor can treat people, but Ally's doctor and nurse knew how to deceive them. Ally had his own doctor and nurse for his employees. They were on vacation when the girl was hospitalized; he had no choice but to take her to the hospital. That's when a social worker intervened, and the girl did everything to conceal the truth. When she got out of the hospital, she tried to escape the camp. Unfortunately, one of the bodyguards didn't give her that chance. Some of the other girls attempted to escape. They also failed.

Some of the girl's mothers were frantically searching for them, and if it wasn't for Sofa's mother they would never get a chance to see their daughters again. One girl was jealous of Sofa just because she received better treatment from Allicobe than her. She accused Sofa of taking money from a client. Allicobe was a very greedy pimp. He sent Sofa home for three days. When he found out the girl was lying, he suspended her for three weeks without pay. Things like that made the girls wonder if this man had a heart or if he is an animal. But some girls made people wonder. A girl named Lala told her best friend, Sofa, that she was in a relationship with a guy. The reason she loved him so much was because he used to abuse her. When they broke up, she became very depressed. The only way to get past it was to become an escort for Allicobe. Another girl explained to her friend how her mother's boyfriend was abusive toward her. One day a neighbor heard a commotion coming from her mother's house, and she called the cops. When they arrived on the scene, the officers attempted to put the boyfriend under arrest, which led to a scuffle. Unfortunately, this caused the boyfriend's death. A girl got jealous of her boyfriend while he was asleep, so she cut one of his arms, moved to Dakar, and ended up working for Allicobe.

Money can force people into doing strange and dangerous things. That's exactly what happened to Ally's boy.

He was in love with a girl he used for money and sex. He encouraged that girl to become an escort for Allicobe.

One day a nun left the convent, and the head of the monastery searched for her in every place in the capital without any luck. She even reported her disappearance to the police department. During the trial, they had found out the nun left the convent to join Allicobe's team. They also found out she was related to one of Allicobe's drifters. When leaving the camp, they applied a lot of makeup on her face, and she wore tinted sunglasses to disguise her appearance. This drifter kidnapped young girls and boys and forced them to work for his boss. The boys worked as messengers and drug traffickers, and the girls worked as escorts.

Mate was badly beaten by one of the boys and was taken to the hospital for medical attention because he stole his money. When they were fighting, the boy screamed, "Mate, cough up the money!" He told the nurses at the hospital that he got hit by a car while crossing the street near his house, and the driver did not stop. The nurses knew he was telling lies because his shirt was clearly ripped by another person. He was treated and discharged.

27

Having said that, some boys and girls were disappointed and were ready to confront Allicobe, but they were not eager to pursue the complaints because the threats were so great, most importantly their lives and the lives of their families that could be put in danger. Looking back, I don't think they knew the situation they were in, like it or not it was a dead end.

A feeling of guilt embraced Mate's body. He started weeping like he had just lost a very important member of his family, like his mother. The next day, he went to talk to Allicobe about his resignation. But Allicobe did not accept his resignation, because he was his right hand, and he made the most money trafficking drugs and kidnapping young boys and girls. Ally threw an employee of the year party for Mate to make him feel appreciated, and everything fell into place.

The drifters distinguished themselves as people with strength and knowledge to beat the streets so they could reach their goals. When you want to succeed in life, your best thing to do is to engage in what you think could help you progress. Don't look for quick money that could disappear within an hour or two. Or become an opportunist by trying to get advantage of innocent girls and boys, that wouldn't look good in the eyes of God and the society.

CHAPTER 5

Mate, the most aggressive drifter, was a father of four kids ranging from eight to three. When they asked at the trial, "Why didn't you think of treating children of others the same way you treat your own?"

He replied, "It was a job like any other." He described how he treated them—like any piece of furniture without sentimental values. "Life is so complex sometimes. I am asking myself where this complexity is taking me."

"I haven't found any answers yet, but I am hopeful," said one of the girls. It seemed like she knew she was out of place, but money and hanging out with rich people who were not on her level made her think and search for answers.

Allicobe had four maids employed in his mansion. They were always arguing over what was going on in his mansion, but they never had the courage to confront their boss. "The money was great," said one.

"But we have no conscience," replied another.

The third said, "I have a family to feed."

The fourth replied, "I don't care about the money. I am just afraid of losing my life and my family."

"If we all report the crimes, I would hope the police department would give us protection."

The first maid said, "What if the police department was an accomplice of Allicobe? Because so many anonymous phone calls were made to the police department, no investigation was conducted."

The second maid said, "If we don't have the courage to come forward, we must leave it alone, or we might end up hurting each other, and life will go on for Allicobe."

One day, while a housekeeper was cleaning some rooms in Allicobe's mansion, a heavy woven cloth with decorative designs used as a wall hanging caught fire. She was sent home for three weeks without pay. When the fire department arrived, they almost caught two girls that a drifter brought to the mansion. Thanks to the gardener's ability, they were safe, and he took them home. The gardener was raised in that mess since the age of three, when his mother was hired as a cook by Allicobe.

He didn't know any better. For some reason, he loved Allicobe and would do anything to protect him. According to the workers, Allicobe had treated Julius like his son. He enrolled him in school, and after he graduated high school Allicobe sent him to a landscaping school, where he had acquired his diploma. The judge asked him to make a comment about the situation. He replied, "I was devastated when they arrested Uncle Ally, but what is fair is fair." He shook his head. "This was how he called him. I knew something was going on, but not to that extent. He treated me very well over the years; it was hard for me to turn him into the authorities. The only thing I had to do was not get involved, and I didn't."

The judge called the gardener, "The right kid in a wrong crib," and he gave him immunity. A look of satisfaction fell on Allicobe's face after the judge gave Julius immunity.

He organized huge parties for the girls so he could introduce them to his rich friends. He hired bands from other countries, like England and America, to entertain them at the party. When Sofa refused to work, he physically abused her. Allicobe had been verbally abusive toward her by telling her, "You are not pretty. This is the reason you did not make it in the fashion industry." He got her pregnant at the age of seventeen. Sofa gave birth to a handsome baby boy. Sofa and the other girls were also abused by Allicobe's rich friends. Incest ran in Allicobe's circle. One of the twelve girls had sex with one of Allicobe's friends, who was her cousin. This was unintentional, because they didn't know each other. One grew up in South Dakar, and the other was born in West Dakar.

CHAPTER 6

>◄═►◄─

For an Independence Day celebration, Allicobe went to visit some family members. He left a pastor in charge of the girls. Three of the pastors were married with children, and some of the girls were Christians. His wife found out he was making a deal for a girl to meet with one of Allicobe's friends, and she left him. At the trial, she testified in court against her husband.

Another pastor kidnapped a girl from his church, and he put her to work for Allicobe. The pastor kicked his wife out of his mansion just because she told him that was wrong, and on top of that she found out he fell in love with the girl. He threatened to hurt her if she reported him to the police. A woman confessed that one of the men abducted a sixteen-year-old boy and gave him a job as a drug trafficker.

Do you think that the drifters would slow down? No, I don't. These Allicobe drifters in particular were too engaged in doing crimes, it would take them years of rehabilitation to help them live a normal life. The consequences for being evil are severe and even psychopathic. The drifters are master manipulators, they should be punished to the fullest extent of the law. Thus, let's live a simple life.

A governor from the town met one of the girls in a ball that Allicobe threw for them one night. The two got cozy that night, and she became his mistress. He bought her a twenty-four-thousand-acre house, a nice convertible BMW, and he ordered her to quit working for Allicobe. In return, Allicobe received a lump sum amount of money for her head. The governor showered the girl's family with precious gifts. By the word of mouth, his wife discovered the affair, and she divorced him. He paid her millions of dollars in alimony and child support.

Another woman entered the court so drunk that the judge asked the police officer to escort her out, and they discovered she was one of the Allicobe's mistresses. She was so distraught by what was going on in the trial that she started drinking from the first day of the trial until she couldn't take it anymore. She appeared in the courtroom and made a fool of herself. The judge kicked her out of the courtroom. The judge returned with his decision and asked the police officer to get her back in the courtroom so he could find out what was going on in her life. She accused Allicobe of beating and assaulting her almost every day. She was a prisoner in her own house. She let the court know she often sneaked out of the house in order to visit her mother and her father. When she returned, she got the same treatment that she always received—a beating.

The judge said, "It is very upsetting for all these women to succumb to greed and to let these men abuse them in such a manner. I don't fall for that."

Allicobe and his friends made the girls feel like they were in an abyss of shame.

Allicobe and his friends were allegedly charged with corruption, fraud, racketeering, sexual assault, battery, and kidnapping. A wave of sadness broke out in the courtroom, and the silence was profound when an officer read the charges. Everybody in the courtroom looked at one another and chanted, "Alleluia!"

Staring at the criminals, they seemed empty and soulless. Moments later they stood up and pleaded not guilty. This was exactly what the lawyers expected. After they pleaded not guilty, a sense of relief was apparent on Sofa's gorgeous face, accompanied by a sense of achievement. But no one could have been happier than Sofa's mother. Sofia's husband could hardly look at her, and each time he did it was obvious that he condemned her for pushing it this far. She returned, did not take long to answer back with her look, and whispered to the person sitting next to her, "I have got him."

Sofa explained to the judge what happened to her on a Christmas day, one of Allicobe's best friends requested her for a night. When she got there, the man asked her to perform an act that she thought was too graphic, she refused to do it. The client became very agitated and started beating on her. God gave her the strength to knock out with a chair. Before Sofa left, she called the police. They took him to the hospital and he regained consciousness.

The police didn't even know Sofa was the person behind the call.

Allicobe and his friends were allegedly charger with corruption, fraud, racketeering, sexual assault, battery and kidnapping. A wave of sadness broke out in the courtroom, and the silence was profound when a court officer read the charges. Everybody in the courtroom looked at each other and chanted, "Alleluia!"

The girls' social worker read these sentences at the trial: "The physical mistreatments that the girls had endured at the hands of Allicobe and his friends finally reached an end. They have to pay enormously for that. But the scars left on their minds will probably never heal."

The jury found them guilty of endangering the welfare of minors. They were sentenced to sixty-five years in prison without the possibility of parole. Allicobe and his friends had paid a good price for Sofa and the other girls who they mistreated. Sofa was awarded three quarters of Allicobe's estate; the other quarter was divided among the other girls and the boys. Sofa, her boyfriend, her mother, her siblings, and the other girls were satisfied with the outcome of the trial. After the verdict, the judge asked

Allicobe if he had anything to say to the girls' families. He replied "I grew up right. My parents were separated over money and left everything in my name at the age of eighteen. Since then, I took money seriously, and I swore I was going to worship it like my god. But now I realize money isn't everything; it can make or break you. The saddest part is, I felt short, and I am sorry for all I have done to your families."

Actually, Allicobe lied to the judge. He wasn't born with money, he portrayed himself differently. He was a son of a debt collector named Salom at the municipal building. He lived in a small village situated fifty miles North of Dakar called Kaolack where people had to work to put food on their table. Allicobe's mother was a fruit picker named Sally. She had a good reputation, and earned the respect of the people in the village. Growing up, Allicobe did not have a good image, he was expelled from school at the age of 15. Allicobe inherited his father's character in a way that the people of the village called him a rude boy. He had to leave the region to relocate to Dakar. He turned the country upside down and was in search of a solid contact that could help him survive for a period of recognition and drive in the business. There he met Mate who became his right hand. Luckily, Mate introduced Allicobe to an investor named Leon who lend him money to become a street vendor. Allicobe couldn't be happier from the start, because he had gotten a deal from a total stranger. Very often only bad people could be that lucky. From then on he opened his first restaurant and hired two girls as escorts. The business grew and everything was history.

Allicobe's mother Sally was not a big woman, but she was not weak either. When her husband Salom died she kept on working even harder to provide for Allicobe. Sally was a good worker at the farm. When the farm owner was about to die and his children wanted to relocate to the city, they arranged for Sally to buy the farm. Fighting on her own, Sally also couldn't keep up with the farm, because Allicobe didn't want to help her; he had something else in mind. Sally had to sell the farm. Still she didn't make the million Alllicobe was talking at the trial. She couldn't save much. Do you think Salom and Sally could leave a million for Alli? No.

Sally was exhausted between her job at the farm and Allicobe's behavior, she became really depressed. She struggled to survive, she eventually sold it. As time went on, one day after her illness progressed and she passed away. Allicobe's mother did her best to raise him, but her best wasn't good enough. With her only son Sally was seeing red, but kept her head high especially, where she got the trust and the respect of the whole neighborhood for being the strong woman she had always been.

After the trial, Sofia served her estranged husband with divorce papers while serving time in prison for the mistreatment she suffered at his hands over the years. His estate was awarded to Sofia and her daughter.

CHAPTER 7

–•◦•–

Sofa, her boyfriend, her mother's five siblings, her grandmother, her grandfather, and her mother were relocated to the largest mansion in Dakar. They hired architects to remodel the mansion. They also hired fashion designers from America, France, London, Senegal, and Dakar to organize a big party to close the case. At the party, Sofa and her boyfriend became engaged. The boyfriend said, "Sofa, the love of my life, would you marry me?"

Sofia replied, "Without a doubt, my love. Despite all that happened in our lives, I always knew this moment would come. Yes."

Three months later, they were married. The pastor asked them, "Ladies and gentlemen, I am here to unite Miss Sofa and Mister Ropy in the institution of marriage. When God created Adam, He did not stop right there. According to him, something else needed to be done. He took a rib from Adam and created Eve. Then he commanded them to be fruitful and to love each other until death do them part. According to Genesis 2:24, 'Therefore, shall a man leave his father and his mother, and shall live unto his wife, and they shall be one flesh.' If anybody in this room thinks this marriage should not take place, please stand. I now pronounce you husband and wife. You may kiss the bride."

At the wedding ceremony, Sofa, her husband, her mother, and the other girls gave themselves to Jesus Christ.

The sacrament of marriage is a very serious sacrament according to Genesis 1:27 to 28 to keep your marriage, it must have a give and take. And never sleep hungry with each other, it depends on the gravity of the problem, but remember there is always a solution to any problems.

After the wedding, Sofa and her husband went to Paris for their honeymoon. They visited the Eiffel Tower, The

Louvre Museum, The Versailles Palace, and Les Champs Elysees. They also went to Italy. They visited The Cinque Terre and Portovenere. The panorama of those places gave them a feeling of wellness.

In conclusion, to live a better life, you have to closely follow the daily events that occur, good or bad but reject the bad and embrace the good. Finally, you will have the best path to follow. I hope that readers learn some valuable lessons from Allicobe and his accomplices. I also hope that they learn some valuable lessons from Sofia and her daughter Sofa's exceptional achievements. Because patience and faith work together to help you live life to its fullest.

CAST MEMBERS

1. the writer (Marie C.)
2. three kidnapped boys
3. four bodyguards
4. two fake priests
5. six clients (Ally's friends)
6. Sofa (Sofia's daughter)
7. Mr. Ropy (Sofa's husband)
8. Mrs. Lagrange (Sofia's mother)
9. Mr. Lagrange (Sofia's father)
10. June (Sofia's rival)
11. Sofia's six brothers and sisters
12. Uncle Bill's love child
13. the judge

14. Miss Lilly (Sofia's patient)

15. Miss Lolita (Miss Lilly's mother)

16. Allicobe (the rich pimp)

17. Gilles (Allicobe's wife)

18. June, Josie, and Lola (Allicobe's mistresses)

19. the three teachers

20. Allicobe's three nieces and nephews

21. Allicobe's son and daughter

22. five drifters and three married pastors (Allicobe's rich friends)

23. a client's wife

24. a nun

25. the governor (child of the governor, his wife, and his mistress)

26. a pastor (Sofa's father's common-law wife)

27. four maids

28. the police department

29. the gardener (Julius)

30. the cook (mother of the gardener)

31. the social worker (for the hospitalized girl)

32. the social worker (for the girls and boys)

33. the pastor (to celebrate the wedding)

34. the musicians

35. the songs

36. the singers

37. the entertainer

Printed in the United States
by Baker & Taylor Publisher Services